Class 2-Much
Makes Money

written by Nadia Vegas

illustrated by Diane Paterson

 McGraw-Hill
School Division

New York   Farmington

Ms. Andrews was the teacher of Class 2-B. Or, as Ms. Andrews would say, Class 2-Much.

The class knew Ms. Andrews's rules. They listened when Ms. Andrews spoke. Even Sue did, sometimes.

Class 2-Much had been learning about tigers. A new baby tiger had just been born at the zoo. The class just had to see it before it got too big.

But they had already been on a field trip in the fall. The school couldn't pay for another trip this spring.

Ms. Andrews's class was very upset, especially Sue. Tigers were her favorite animals.

Over the weekend, everyone in Ms. Andrews's class thought about how to raise money for the trip. On Monday morning they told Ms. Andrews their ideas.

Will thought of having a bake sale. Alice wanted to put on a music show. Kisha said they should collect cans. Marcus suggested holding a race.

But Sue didn't like any of those ideas.

"I think we should sell ice cream," said
Sue. Ice cream was her favorite food.

"But we don't have a place to keep it
cold," Will pointed out.

"And nobody likes to eat melted ice
cream," said Pablo.

Sue frowned. "I do," she thought.

Then Ms. Andrews started writing on the board.

"We'll do it the right way," she announced. "We'll make a list."

"Who would buy a list?" asked Sue.

Ms. Andrews continued to write on the board. Then she read the first question. "What can we make on our own?" she asked.

The class was quiet. Everyone was thinking.

Suddenly Luke called out, "I've got it!"

He pointed to the calendar on the wall.

"Why would we make calendars?" said Sue. "It's already May."

"But look at how many birthdays there are this month," said Luke. "We can make birthday cards."

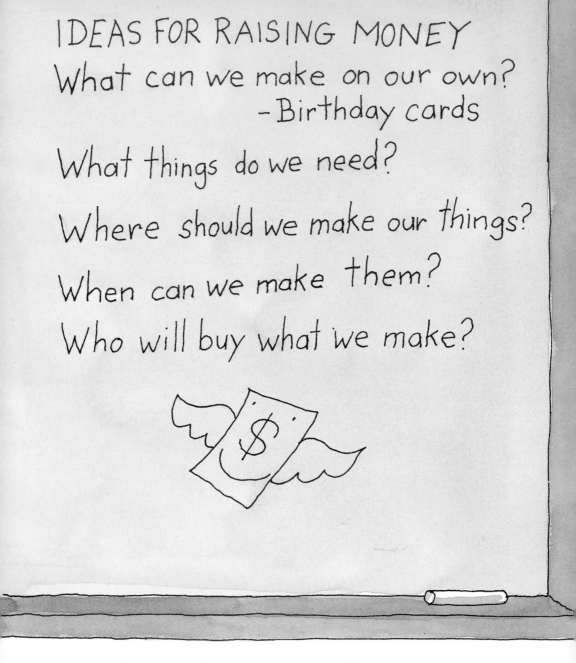

IDEAS FOR RAISING MONEY
What can we make on our own?
                              - Birthday cards

What things do we need?

Where should we make our things?

When can we make them?

Who will buy what we make?

Ms. Andrews smiled. She wrote the answer to the first question on the list.

The class was very excited. They began making a lot of plans. Or, as Ms. Andrews would say, a lot of noise.

-Art Supplies

One by one, the class answered each question on the list.

They already had plenty of art supplies.

They could make the cards in the classroom after school each day.

And they would sell the cards to the parents who were coming to see the school play.

Class 2-Much started the very next day. It was Tuesday, and they had only a few days left before the play on the following Monday night.

Ms. Andrews set up a big space in the room. The class cut and folded cardboard, then cut and folded some more. They made hundreds of blank cards.

After school on Wednesday, Ms. Andrews poured some paint into bowls.

"Oh good," said Sue. "This is the fun part. The messy part."

Class 2-Much worked fast. Soon the bowls were empty. The front of each card was covered in a rainbow of colors.

So was Sue.

On Thursday afternoon, Kisha and
Luke brought in letter stamps and ink
pads.

Sue said, "I was wrong. This is the
messy part."

Soon each card was stamped with
the words HAPPY BIRTHDAY in lots
of colors.

So was Sue.

On Friday came the messiest part of all.

"Yes!" Sue yelled when she saw the glue, glitter, and silver markers.

The class used rulers to draw silver lines around each card. Then they squeezed glue along the edges and dipped them in glitter.

Sue looked like she had been dipped in glitter, too.

On Monday, the class was ready for the
last step. They made packs of five cards
with five envelopes. They tied each pack
with blue string. The cards were beautiful!

That evening Class 2-Much brought a
huge box to the play. They set up a booth
by the ticket line. Sue made sure
everyone knew about it.

"Yahoo!" Sue yelled, "and whoop-de-do!
Birthday cards for you and you! Two
dollars a pack. Buy one or buy two!"

All the packs sold out in a flash. They
were such a hit that the class planned
to make more cards in June.

And the next week, Class 2-Much got to see the baby tiger at the zoo.

The trip was really great. Or, as Ms. Andrews would say, really too much!